D0099477

Harry Potter™

POSTER BOOK

THE WORLD OF
HARRY POTTER

SCHOLASTIC INC.

New York   Toronto   London   Auckland   Sydney
Mexico City   New Delhi   Hong Kong

No part of this publication may be reproduced in whole or in part,
or stored in a retrieval system, or transmitted in any form or by any means,
electronic, mechanical, photocopying, recording, or otherwise,
without written permission of the publisher.
For information regarding permission, write to Scholastic Inc.,
Attention: Permissions Department, 557 Broadway, New York, NY 10012.

ISBN 978-0-545-31213-4

Copyright © 2011 by Warner Bros. Entertainment Inc.
HARRY POTTER characters, names and related indicia are trademarks of and
© Warner Bros. Entertainment Inc.
Harry Potter Publishing Rights © J. K. Rowling.
(s11)

All rights reserved. Published by Scholastic Inc.
SCHOLASTIC and associated logos
are trademarks and/or registered trademarks of Scholastic Inc.

12 11 10 9 8 7 6 5 4 3 2 1   11 12 13 14 15 16/0

Art Direction by Rick DeMonico
Book Design by Heather Barber

Printed in Singapore First printing, June 2011   46

CONTENTS

PART I
LIFE AT HOGWARTS™

STUDENT PORTRAITS

Harry Potter™

Hermione Granger™

Ron Weasley™

Ginny Weasley™

Fred & George Weasley

Neville Longbottom™

Seamus Finnigan

Dean Thomas

Romilda Vane

Cormac McLaggen

Lavender Brown™

Padma Patil

Parvati Patil

Draco Malfoy™

Vincent Crabbe

Gregory Goyle

Blaise Zabini

Cedric Diggory

43

Cho Chang

RAVENCLAW

Luna Lovegood™

RAVENCLAW

HOGWARTS CASTLE AND GROUNDS

Hogwarts Castle

The Fat Lady

Library

The Great Hall

The Chamber of Secrets™

Gryffindor™ common room

Corridors and staircases

Quidditch™ pitch

Potions classroom

Hospital wing

Room of Requirement

Whomping Willow

Slytherin™ common room

Owlery

Hagrid's hut

Forbidden Forest

STAFF AT HOGWARTS™

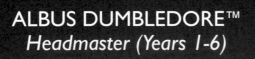

ALBUS DUMBLEDORE™
Headmaster (Years 1-6)

MINERVA McGONAGALL™
Deputy Headmistress, Transfiguration teacher,
Head of Gryffindor house

RUBEUS HAGRID™
Keeper of Keys and Grounds and
Care of Magical Creatures teacher

SEVERUS SNAPE™
Headmaster (Year 7), Defense Against the Dark Arts
teacher and Head of Slytherin house

FILIUS FLITWICK
Charms teacher and
Head of Ravenclaw house

ARGUS FILCH
Caretaker

MADAM POMFREY
Hospital wing matron

SIBYLL TRELAWNEY
Divination teacher

HORACE SLUGHORN
Potions master

POMONA SPROUT
*Herbology teacher and
Head of Hufflepuff house*

MADAM HOOCH
Flying teacher and Quidditch referee

DEFENSE AGAINST THE DARK ARTS TEACHERS

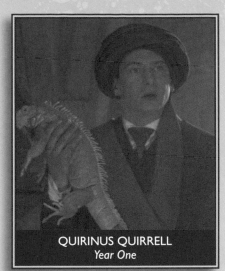

QUIRINUS QUIRRELL
Year One

GILDEROY LOCKHART™
Year Two

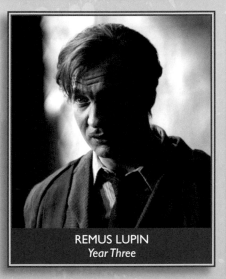

REMUS LUPIN
Year Three

ALASTOR "MAD-EYE" MOODY
Year Four

DOLORES UMBRIDGE™
Year Five

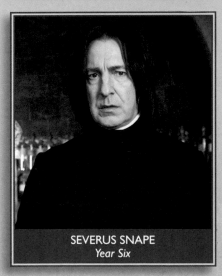

SEVERUS SNAPE
Year Six

STUDENT LIFE

DUMBLEDORE'S ARMY

QUIDDITCH™

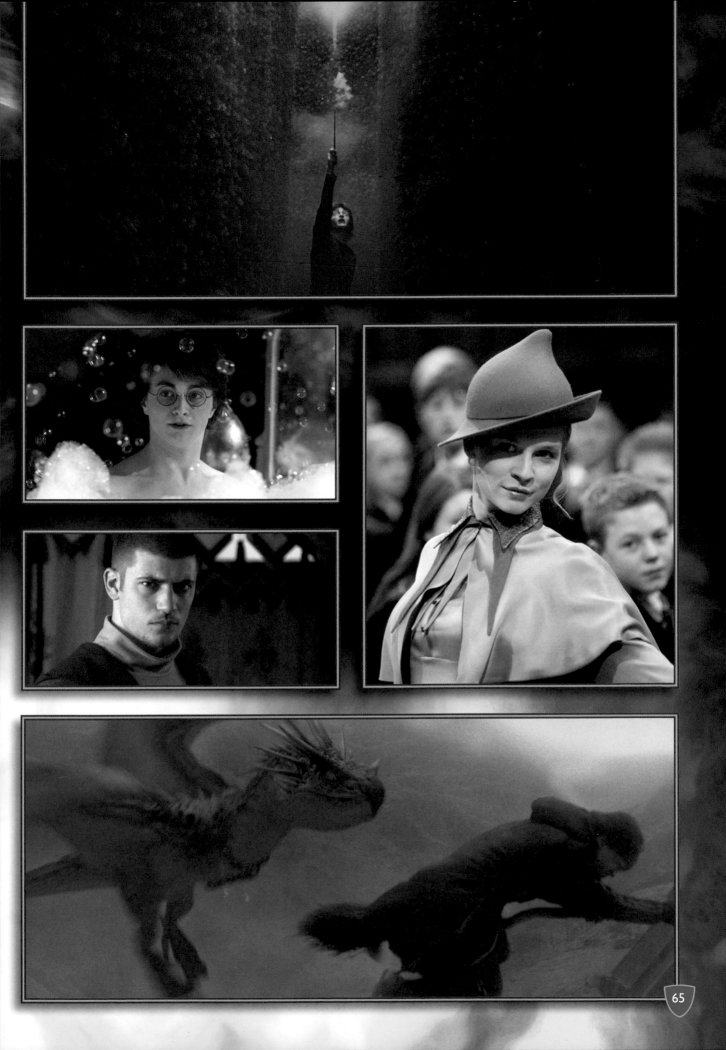

THROUGH THE YEARS

PART II
THE WIZARDING WORLD

THE MINISTRY OF MAGIC

Ministry of Magic elevator

Visitors' entrance to the Ministry of Magic

Wizengamot

Atrium

Hall of Prophecy

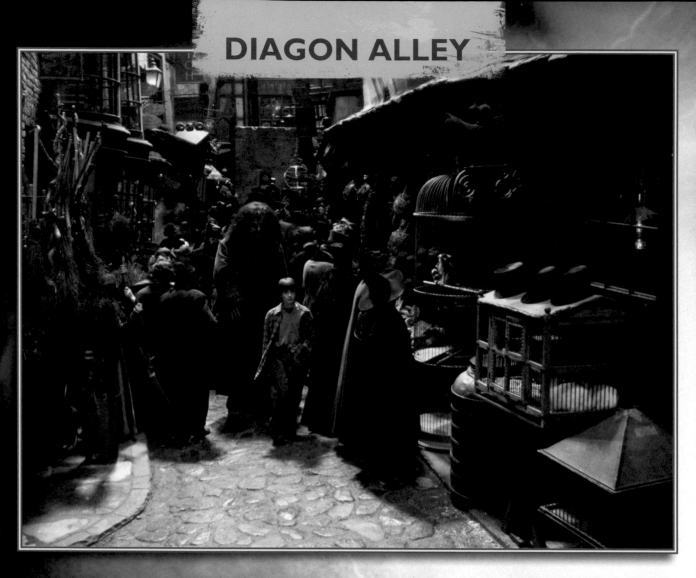

Weasleys' Wizard Wheezes

Eeylops Owl Emporium

Ollivanders

Gringotts

93

Hogsmeade High Street

Shrieking Shack

Hog's Head

Honeydukes

MAGICAL CREATURES

Fawkes™ the phoenix

Dementor

Basilisk

Dobby™ the house-elf

Werewolf

Goblin

Thestral

Buckbeak™ the Hippogriff

Hungarian Horntail dragon

PART III

BATTLING DARK FORCES

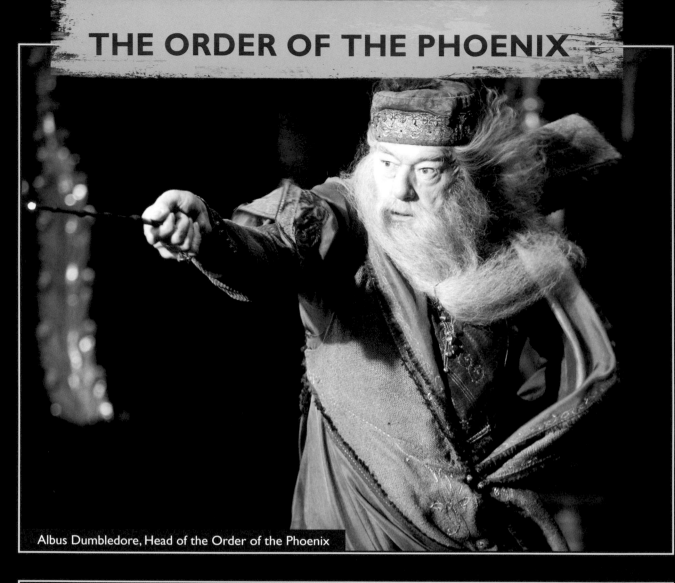

Albus Dumbledore, Head of the Order of the Phoenix

Severus Snape

Remus Lupin

Sirius Black™

101

Arthur Weasley

Molly Weasley

Fred and George Weasley

Bill Weasley and Fleur Delacour

Kingsley Shacklebolt

Alastor "Mad-Eye" Moody

Nymphadora Tonks™

Minerva McGonagall

103

Lord Voldemort™

Bellatrix Lestrange

Lucius Malfoy

Draco Malfoy

Fenrir Greyback

Barty Crouch Jr.

Peter Pettigrew

Narcissa Malfoy

Scabior

EPIC
MOMENTS

FACING THE BASILISK

VOLDEMORT RETURNS

BATTLE AT THE BURROW

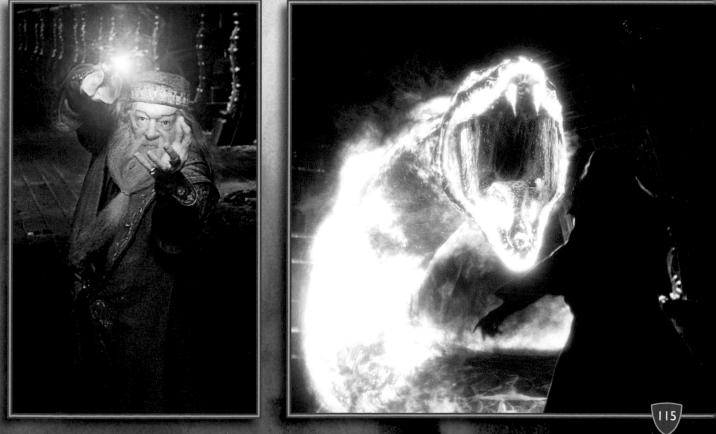

BREAKING INTO GRINGOTTS